Written by
Barbara Swisher Amundson

Illustrated by
Alejandra Barajas

STANLEY'S
STANDING OVATION!

Copyright ©2024 Barbara Swisher Amundson

Written by Barbara Swisher Amundson
Illustrations by Alejandra Barajas

Photograph of Barbara Swisher Amundson by Ireland Jones Photography

Published by Miriam Laundry Publishing Company
miriamlaundry.com

All rights reserved. This book or any portion thereof may not be reproduced or used in any manner whatsoever without the express written permission from the author except for the use of brief quotations in a book review.

HC ISBN 978-1-77944-099-0
PB ISBN 978-1-77944-098-3
e-Book ISBN 978-1-77944-097-6

FIRST EDITION

Dedication:

To Gabe and Emmett, my sweet grandchildren who are the inspiration for this children's picture book and who inspire my creative imagination every day.

Also, to dear grandchildren Ireland, Bryn, Joel, Katie, Liam, Elle, Evelin, Charlotte, Grace, and Caroline whose sweetness and love also continues to fill my heart.

Thank you to my children Todd and Tyler Despins and my parents Frank and Marie Scheirich for your constant presence and love throughout my life.

A sincere thank you to my English teachers throughout the years. Your wisdom and encouragement inspired my love of literature and composition.

And finally, to my dear husband Kevin, whose support and love is unwavering and everything to me. Thank you for being on this and life's journey with me.

Emmett & Gabe

On Friday afternoon, the school principal makes an announcement.

"Attention! Attention students!" Mrs. Vanderloo booms with a friendly voice.

"Monday is the Bonnerville Elementary School Science Fair. You have the weekend to build a project, and the winner will be announced at the science fair. Have fun!"

Stanley and his little brother Alfie giggle and tease each other all the way home from school. Alfie throws his jacket on the front step and runs to get their bikes. Stanley is quiet. He is thinking and wondering about a science project.

"Okay. See you later, Stanley."

Stanley stares at his bike.
He spins the wheels and
watches the spokes.
"I wonder..." he whispers.

"Hey, Stanley!" Alfie shouts. "Come climb the rock wall with me! I made it all the way to the top last time."

Stanley's knees start to shake as he remembers the last time he climbed the rock wall.

"No, Alfie," says Stanley. "I don't want to climb the rock wall today."

"Okay, Stanley."

Stanley stares at the rock garden in the front yard. He pulls out some loose rocks and piles them one on top of the other. "I wonder..." he whispers.

"Hey, Stanley!" Alfie shouts. "Come skipping with me!"
He hands Stanley the skipping rope.

Stanley's legs start to wobble as he remembers the last time he tried jump rope.
"No, Alfie," says Stanley, rubbing his ankle.
"I don't want to skip today."

"Okay," Alfie replies. "See you later!"

Stanley stares at the skipping rope. He begins to twist it into knots.
"I wonder..." he whispers.

"Hey, Stanley!" Alfie shouts. "Come fly your kite with us!" Stanley tries to fly his kite, but it dives to the ground. Stanley's face feels hot.

"No, Alfie!" cries Stanley. "There is no wind over here. I don't want to fly my kite today."

Stanley watches the other kites. Suddenly, he sees a flock of geese flying overhead. "Wow!" Stanley says. "They're in a perfect V! How do geese do that?"

Stanley runs home and gets out his triangle ruler. He begins to draw. "I wonder..." whispers Stanley.

"Hey, Stanley!" Alfie screams. Alfie charges down the field, looking over his shoulder. "Pass me the ball!"

Stanley kicks the ball to Alfie and lands face down in the grass.

"It's okay, Alfie," shouts a teary-eyed Stanley. "I don't want to play ball right now."

Stanley stares at something moving in the grass. He watches in amazement at fourteen ants going up and down on an ant hill. They are building an ant city.

Stanley runs home. He grabs his collection of popsicle sticks and glue. "I wonder..." he whispers.

"Hey, Stanley!" Alfie calls.
Alfie runs and jumps on the merry-go-round as it starts to pick up speed. "Are you coming for a ride?"

Stanley remembers he felt dizzy and queasy the last time he went round and round on the merry-go-round.

"No, Alfie!" Stanley yells. "I don't want to ride the merry-go-round today!"

Stanley watches as the merry-go-round goes round and round in a circle.
He thinks, *Why does that middle post stay still?* When the ride stops, it then moves backward in a circle.

Stanley runs home.
He digs out his colored pens and spiral art gears.
"I wonder..." he whispers.

"Hey, Stanley!" Alfie screams.
Alfie jumps into a cardboard box and tumbles down the hill, almost bumping into other children. "Whoa!" Alfie laughs as he rolls out of the box at the bottom of the hill.
He tosses Stanley his old box.
"I'm done. Want to take a turn, Stanley?"

Stanley's heart begins to pound as he remembers the last time he rolled down the hill in a box.

"No, Alfie!" Stanley answers, rubbing the back of his head. "I don't want to slide down the hill in a box today."

Stanley stares at the old box beside him.
It is bent and torn.
Stanley picks it up and runs home.

He grabs scissors and
tape off his desk.
"I wonder..." he whispers.

Stanley stays up late working.
His desk is covered with all sorts
of drawings and materials.
"I think it might work," whispers Stanley.
He yawns and finally crawls into bed.

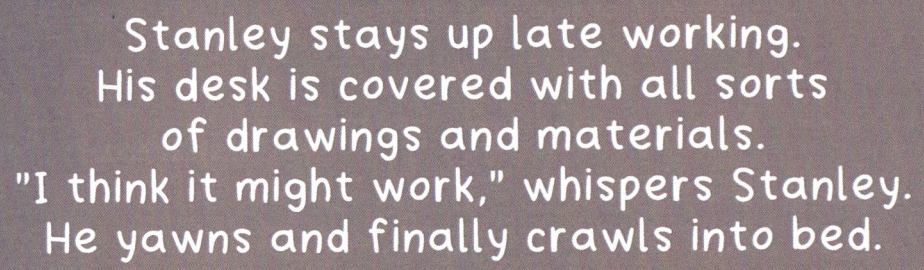

His little brother Alfie has been asleep for hours.

On Monday, the Bonnerville Elementary School gymnasium is filled with students and teachers and family.

Everyone oohs and aahs as they look at the science projects.
Mrs. Vanderloo moves from project to project, frowning and nodding and making notes.

Stanley stands in front of his project.
Mrs. Vanderloo stops and stares.
"Hmmm," she mutters, before moving on.

Mrs. Vanderloo steps to the microphone.
Her voice booms out.
"ATTENTION! ATTENTION PLEASE!
Thank you, students, for your wonderful projects!
Very well done!

AND...THE WINNER OF THE BONNERVILLE ELEMENTARY SCHOOL SCIENCE PROJECT IS..."

Everyone begins clapping
and cheering,
for Stanley has built a most
miraculous project—a rope bridge
with wheels and pulleys too.

"STANLEY.
THE WINNER
IS
STANLEY!!"

Stanley is rushed to the center of the stage
to a loud 'Standing Ovation.'
Stanley feels dizzy.
His heart races and his face feels hot.
But this time,
Stanley is smiling ear to ear.

Stanley and Alfie giggle and tease each other all the way home from school.
Alfie throws his jacket on the front step and sits down beside Stanley.
"Don't you want to play something?" Stanley asks.

"No, Stanley," replies Alfie. "I don't want to play something. I want you to teach me to build something."

"Okay, Alfie." Stanley smiles. "Let's go find something to build!"

Printed in the USA
CPSIA information can be obtained
at www.ICGtesting.com
LVRC080731280824
789500LV00010B/54